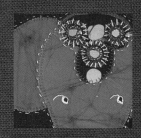

EXCUSE ME, IS THIS INDIA?

Anita Leutwiler
Anushka Ravishankar

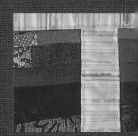

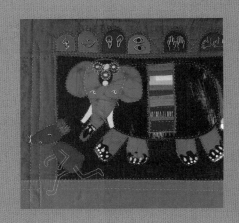

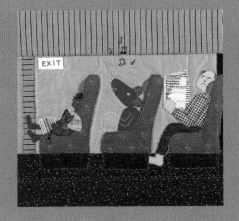

My Aunt Anna came back from India
With stories of places to which she had been.
To warm me through winter, she sewed me a quilt
With pictures of all the things she had seen.

I looked at the pictures and secretly thought,
That one day I'd see all the places and things
Which were in the quilt that my Aunt Anna brought:
Elephants, bandicoots, crows with black wings.

At bedtime I snuggled in under my quilt,
But just at the moment I closed my eyes
I suddenly became a bright blue mouse,
And soon I was in for a bigger surprise ...

I was sitting in an aeroplane
High up in the air.
A man who sat beside me asked
With a friendly stare:

"Where do you think you're going?
And what will you do there?"
"I'm sorry Sir," I said to him,
"I don't know where this goes."
"You only have," he pointed out,
"To follow your own nose."

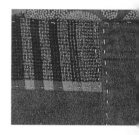

So when we landed finally,
I followed my nose to the sea.

A cow stood on the sunny beach,
Eating paper from a bin.
I went to her and asked her, "Ma'am,
Which country am I in?"

"It's East of this and North of that
And South-west of the other."
At this four crows that stood around
Began to caw together.

"It's East!" "It's South!"
"It's North!" "It's West!"
They circled round my head.

I put a sea-shell to my ear
To hear the sea instead.

I saw a girl outside her house,
I thought we could be friends.
"Where am I?" I asked her.
She replied, "That depends."

She drew a map without a place
And said, "Let me explain the case:
If you were standing on your head
I'd say you're on your hair.
But since you're standing on your feet
You could be anywhere."

I left her with a silent sigh,
She waved her broom to say goodbye.

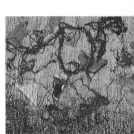

I met two furry bandicoots
Running in the garden.
"Excuse me," I called to them.
They answered, "Beg your pardon?"

"Could you tell me where I am?
And where I ought to go?"
They twitched their noses and they said,
"We're sorry, we don't know.

We might be at the Equator,
Or even the North Pole.
It doesn't matter much to us,
We live inside a hole."

Just outside a temple gate
Stood an elephant.
"Off with your shoes!
Off with your shoes!"
He blared to all who went.

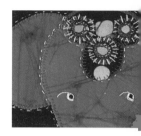

"Please help me, Sir," I said to him,
"I really need to know:
Where it is that I have come
And how I have to go."

"First left then right then up then down
Then back then forth then here then there
Then to then fro ..." he carried on,
I ran away in great despair.

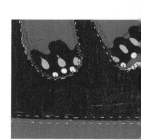

I hopped into a three-wheeled car
And called out, "Take me there!"
The driver started off at once,
He never asked me 'Where?'

Suddenly he stopped and said,
"At last we're getting near."
"Near to what?" I asked him.
He bellowed in my ear:
"Near to this is far from that!
I think that's very clear!"

Though it wasn't clear to me,
I nodded very cleverly.

Ramaram Silks

At a shop I stopped to see
If I could get a hint
Of where I was, but all I saw
Were clothes of every tint.

"Where am I and what's this place?"
I asked of everyone.
A woman came and said to me,
"You're as far as you can run.
But if you learn to fly, then you
Could catch up with the sun."

I left the shop
With a happy hop.

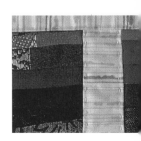

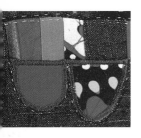

I hopped until the airport
And there! There was a sign.
But suddenly I realised
I couldn't read a line.

I asked a bearded gentleman.
He said, "Oh don't you know?
It doesn't matter where you are
But where you want to go."

I sat down there
And scratched my head,
And thought of what
The man had said.

I jumped into an aeroplane
And got prepared to fly.
But a gloomy person said to me,
"We'll never reach the sky.

The pilot says this plane has got
A very stubborn wing.
It only flies if somebody
Will continuously sing."

I sang a long and endless song
With a silly tune.
I wondered where I was going now
And whether I'd reach soon.

I opened my eyes and found it was morning,
It was only a dream and I was in bed.
Outside my window, I saw it was snowing,
All that had happened was inside my head.

I looked at Aunt Anna's quilt and I thought,
One day I'll get on a real aeroplane,
And fly off to India like Aunt Anna did,
And see all those people and places again.

Excuse me, is this India?

First published in India by Tara Publishing

Copyright ©2001 Tara Publishing
For the illustrations: Anita Leutwiler

Second printing: 2003

For this edition (2005):

Tara Publishing Ltd., UK <www.tarabooks.com/uk>
and
Tara Publishing, India <www.tarabooks.com>

Design: minus9 design

Production: C. Arumugam

ISBN: 81-86211-56-X

Anita Leutwiler is a Swiss textile artist who lives in Germany. When she travelled to India in 1999, she collected bits and pieces of the amazing textile riches of the country. The pictures she created are a unique memory of her trip. Anita would like to dedicate the book to her supportive husband, Heinz.

Anushka Ravishankar is an Indian writer who has written several books of absurd verse for children. She was inspired by Anita's pictures to create a fantastic story of travel in a child's imagination.